The Riding Lesson

Written by
Susan Williamson

Illustrated by
CJ McGannon

HighTide
Publications, Inc.

High Tide Publications, Inc.

1000 Bland Point

Deltaville, Virginia 23043

www.hightidepublications.com

First Edition

ISBIN: 978-1-945990-54-0

For Stella, my Beta reader
and
Buttons, the best lesson pony ever

Chapter 1

Sadie was watching out the window while her mother fixed dinner. "Daddy's home," she said.

Her father walked in and gave her a big hug. "How was school today?" he asked.

"It was good. What are we doing tomorrow?"

"Hmm, are you going to school?"

"No, silly. Tomorrow is Saturday."

"Did you ask Mom?"

"Yes, but she said it was a surprise. My birthday is tomorrow, you know."

"It is? Let's see, will you be seven?"

"No, Daddy, I'm already seven, I will be eight. Old enough to have a pony, or maybe even a horse."

In fact, Sadie had been asking for a pony for her birthday and for Christmas as long as she could remember. Her parents told her that they didn't have any place to keep a pony. But she knew that her friend Heidi had a pony that her parents boarded at a big barn.

Her mother looked up from the pot of spaghetti she was cooking. "I guess you will just have to wait until tomorrow to find out the surprise."

Sadie didn't give up. She kept asking questions. "What do I wear for the surprise?"

"That's part of the surprise," her mother said, "now get ready for bed and tomorrow will be here before you know it."

Sadie read her favorite book before bed. It was about a girl and her horse.

Chapter 2

Sunlight was coming through the window. "It's my birthday!" she thought and ran downstairs.

Dad was cooking pancakes. Yummy. He even put chocolate chips in them. Sadie looked around and saw some wrapped presents on the couch in the family room.

"Are those for me?"

"Of course," her mother said as she walked into the room wearing jeans and a sweater. But you can't open them yet."

Sadie ate her pancakes and then her mother told her to get dressed. "What should I wear?"

"Oh jeans will be fine, and your tennis shoes ."

Were they going to the park? Sadie loved the park, but they went there a lot. A trip to the park wouldn't be a birthday surprise would it?

Sadie remembered to brush her teeth and her hair and then she grabbed her jacket and climbed into the back seat. She noticed that her presents were in the car also.

They drove down the street and turned away from town, out toward the country. Sadie didn't know this road. Maybe it went to a park with rides. That would be fun.

"Can you tell me where we are going?" Sadie asked.

"Nope, but we're almost there."

Chapter 3

Mom slowed the car and turned into a driveway with a board fence and horses grazing in the pasture. "I see horses!" Sadie yelled.

Her mom parked the car and said, "Now I think it is time to open some of your presents."

Dad handed her a square box. She opened it and found a riding helmet. She looked up at her dad with a big smile.

"We decided that you are old enough to take riding lessons," he said.

"You'll need this too," her mom said and handed her another present to open. Inside were shiny riding boots. "Go ahead, put them on."

They walked into the big barn. A pretty lady wearing boots and riding pants came to meet them. "Are you Sadie?" she asked.

Sadie grinned. "Yes."

"I'm Miss Jean. Let's go meet Mr. Buttons."

Buttons was a mostly white pony with brown spots all over his body. "See," she said, "those are his Buttons." Sadie touched Buttons. His coat was soft and very furry. In fact, white hair came off in her hand.

Chapter 4

Miss Jean led Buttons into the arena. She told Sadie to bend her knee and Miss Jean lifted her onto the pony. She adjusted the stirrups and showed Sadie how to hold the reins. "Just make a cluck and ask him to walk," she said.

Sadie tried to make the clucking sound and Buttons started to walk.

Sadie grabbed onto the saddle. "No, Sadie," Miss Jean said, "you can't guide the pony unless you are holding the reins above the saddle." She showed Sadie how to pull the right rein to turn right and the left rein to turn left. Soon Sadie was using her reins to make the pony turn and stop. Her parents were making pictures with their phones. She wanted to wave, but she knew that she was supposed to hold onto the reins all of the time.

Miss Jean asked her, "Do you want to go a little faster? "

Sadie nodded. Miss Jean took ahold of the pony and ran beside him, holding Sadie's leg. It was so bumpy! She giggled.

"It's bouncy isn't it? But I can show you how to go up and down and it won't be so bouncy."

She showed Sadie how to stand up in the

stirrups and sit back down. It was scary to stand up. And she really had to push hard. They practiced while the pony was walking. Then Miss Jean asked the pony to trot. "Up-down, up-down," she said.

Sadie felt like she was going up when she should be going down and when she came down she bounced more than ever. She didn't know it would be this hard. They walked for a while so Sadie could rest and catch her breath.

"Are you ready to trot again?" Miss Jean asked.

Sadie didn't really want to trot any more, but she knew she should try again. "Okay," she said.

At first she was bouncing all over the saddle. But then she listened to Miss Jean. "Push yourself up and let yourself down. Don't just fall down."

Sadie tried to push up with her legs and when Miss Jean said, "Down," she lowered her body. As soon as her bottom touched the saddle, Miss Jean said, "Up."

She began to feel the rhythm of the up and down. Now she wasn't bouncing any more. But her back was starting to hurt.

They rested again. "I think you've got it," Miss Jean said with a smile. "Could you feel it?"

Sadie grinned. "Yes, but it makes my back hurt," she said.

"That's because you're trying so hard. But you will build muscles and it will get better. Horse girls are tough."

Sadie took a deep breath. "Can we trot one more time?"

"You bet," said Ms. Jean.

Sadie was going up and down in time with the horse. It felt wonderful. Before she knew it, Miss Jean was asking her to stop the pony. She told Sadie to take her right leg out of the stirrup and bring it over the pony's back, then slip her left leg out and slide down to the ground.

She gave Buttons lots of pats and Miss Jean showed her how to lead him back to the barn. "Remember to look where you are going, not at the pony."

Chapter 5

Sadie led Buttons into the barn and Miss Jean slipped a halter over his bridle and snapped a rope lead onto the halter. Then she tied the rope to a ring on the wall. Buttons closed his eyes and took a nap.

Miss Jean said, "Next time I'll let you unsaddle him, but he has another lesson later, so we'll leave him here. Did you have fun?"

"Yes," Sadie answered. "Did you say next time?"

"Your parents bought a package of lessons for you, so you will come every Saturday."

Sadie looked at her mom and dad and ran over and hugged them both. "This is the best birthday ever." She said. "Thank you!"

"She did really well for her first lesson," Miss Jean told her parents.

"I know," her mother said. "We are so proud of her."

An older girl walked over to them. "I'm Betsy," she said. "I can show you some of the other horses if you like."

Betsy told her the names of all of the horses

in the barn. A black and white horse whinnied to them. Her name was Katie. A small gray horse was named China. Sadie thought the most beautiful horse was Shasta. She was a copper red color and had a narrow white blaze on her face.

Sadie could have stayed at the barn all day, but her parents said it was time to go eat lunch and she got to pick where, since it was her special day. She chose Panera so she could eat their macaroni and cheese, yum.

The Riding Lesson
Coloring Book

Welcome to our multi-generational coloring book. Some are easy; some are hard.

We hope you will enjoy coloring together.

About the Author

Susan Williamson grew up on a horse and livestock farm in western Pennsylvania. She holds a BS in Animal Science from the University of Kentucky with a certification in Riding Instruction and a MS in Animal Breeding from the University of California at Davis where she was a founding member of the UC Davis Polo Club.

She has worked as a Kentucky 4-H Extension Agent, area Horse specialist and state 4H horse show superintendent. She and her husband operated Williamson Stables, a breeding, boarding, lesson, training and show barn in Kentucky and North Carolina.

Williamson has helped many first time horse buyers and continues to work as a substitute riding instructor and coach.

She is also a groom for competitive driving horses.

About the Illustrator

When CJ McGannon was 4 years old her auntie asked..'what will you be when you grow up'?

CJ thought a moment and said...' I will be a artist...and I will have horses!"

It was a long and winding road, but she did as she said, and believes that you can follow your dreams if you never give up!

CJ has lived in 12 states, 5 countries and visited many others.

She has won awards for fine art , fiber arts , design, and illustration.

She has trained and loved many horses, and taken them to win local championships.

CJ plans to continue making art and loving horses until she is 101!

She hopes you will too!

CPSIA information can be obtained
at www.ICGtesting.com
Printed in the USA
BVHW010449041118
531620BV00002B/11/P